*To Christopher,*
*with love*
T. K.


*For David*
H. O.

Text copyright © 2016 by Timothy Knapman
Illustrations copyright © 2016 by Helen Oxenbury

First U.S. edition 2017

Library of Congress Catalog Card Number pending
ISBN 978-0-7636-9078-6

APS 21 20 19 18 17 16
10 9 8 7 6 5 4 3 2 1

Printed in Humen, Dongguan, China.

This book was typeset in Bodoni Egyptian Pro.
The illustrations were done in pencil and watercolor.

Candlewick Press
99 Dover Street
Somerville, Massachusetts 02144

visit us at www.candlewick.com

# Time Now to Dream

Timothy Knapman    *illustrated by* Helen Oxenbury

CANDLEWICK PRESS

Alice and Jack were out
playing catch when they heard
something that sounded like . . .

Ocka by hay beees
unna da reeees

"What's that noise?" said Jack.

"It's coming from the forest,"
said Alice. "Let's go and see!"

"But what if it's the Wicked Wolf?"
said Jack. "I want to go home."

"Shhh," said Alice. "Everything is
going to be all right."


And she held Jack's hand.

Alice and Jack were stepping into
the forest when they heard something
that sounded like . . .

Offtis or eeef edd
un gentil daa breez

"What's that noise?" said Jack.
"I don't like it."

"Let's go and see," said Alice.

"But what if it's the Wicked Wolf,"
    said Jack, "with his big bad claws?"

"Shhh," said Alice. "Everything is
    going to be all right."

Alice and Jack were creeping through
the forest when they heard something
that sounded like . . .

Ime now to reem
ing de taaars in a sky

"What's that noise?" said Jack.
"We're lost!"

"It's just over there," said Alice.
"Let's go and see."

"What if it's the Wicked Wolf,"
said Jack, "with his big bad claws
and his snap-trap jaws?"

"Shhh," said Alice. "Everything is
going to be all right."

"I want to be home," said Jack.
"I want to be warm and wearing my pajamas.
I want to be snuggled down deep."

"We have to be brave," said Alice.

And that's when they heard it,
very close now.

Sossay to leeep
on mie eeeet ullaby

"It's right in front of us!"
said Jack.

Big bad claws . . .

snap-trap jaws . . .

# THE WICKED WOLF!

"RUN!" cried Alice.

"All the way home!"

But Jack didn't move.

"The Wolf isn't wicked," said Jack.
"The Wolf is a mommy. That's
what the noise is! Mommy Wolf
is singing her babies to sleep!

Look!"

Rock-a-bye, babies,
under the trees.

Soft is your leaf bed
and gentle the breeze.

Time now to dream,
sing the stars in the sky,

So sail off to sleep
on my sweet lullaby.

"Everything is all right," said Jack.
Then he gave a great big yawn.
"It's time to go home."

And he held Alice's hand.

Alice and Jack
walked back through
the forest . . .

and all the way home.

They got into their
nice, warm pajamas and
snuggled down deep.

And they sailed off to sleep
on that sweet lullaby.